W9-CGP-860

Words to Know Before You Read

hurl

launch

pitch

sail

shoot

soar

toss

zing

www.rourkeeducationalmedia.com

Edited by Precious McKenzie
Illustrated by Anita DuFalla
Art Direction and Page Layout by Renee Brady

Library of Congress PCN Data

Table Wars / Kyla Steinkraus
ISBN 978-1-61810-197-6 (hard cover) (alk. paper)
ISBN 978-1-61810-330-7 (soft cover)
Library of Congress Control Number: 2012936798

Rourke Educational Media
Printed in the United States of America,
North Mankato, Minnesota

rourkeeducationalmedia.com

customerservice@rourkeeducationalmedia.com • PO Box 643328 Vero Beach, Florida 32964

By Kyla Steinkraus
Illustrated by Anita DuFalla

Shirley Squirrel liked school. Her favorite part of the school day was lunch.

Every lunch period Shirley sat with her best friends, Lucy Goose and Calypso Cat.

At the next table, Cooper Cub and his friends laughed loudly. Smokey Spaniel placed a walnut on his spoon, bent it back, and shot it across the cafeteria.

The walnut walloped Shirley on the back of her head. "Hey!" she yelped.

"Sorry," Smokey said sheepishly.

Shirley was about to tell him it was okay, but Calypso Cat snatched up string cheese and sent it sailing through the air.

The cheese smacked Ernest Elephant right between the eyes and slid down his trunk!

Tallulah Turtle giggled. “That’s so funny!” she said, just as a bit of bologna bounced off the table and landed in her lap.

“Yuck!” Lucy Goose shrieked as Cooper tossed tomato slices at her. Red juice soaked into her feathers.

"This is war!" Shirley cried, launching her lasagna across the room. The lasagna missed Calypso Cat and splattered noodles and sauce all over Mike and Spike, the two monkeys sitting at the next table.

"Hooray!" cried the monkeys, wiping melted cheese out of their eyes. They pitched their pickles at Shirley and Calypso.

"Please stop!" yelled the lunch lady, Penny Possum. But no one heard her. Everyone shrieked and laughed as pieces of food soared through the air.

Turtles and squirrels catapulted cantaloupes. Cats and dogs zinged zucchinis. And, the elephant hurled avalanches of applesauce.

Finally, all the lunch boxes were empty. Food was splashed over the tables, splattered on clothes, and smashed all over the floor.

Cooper Cub, Tallulah Turtle, and Mike and Spike quickly wiped themselves down and started to leave.

Shirley Squirrel looked across the messy cafeteria and noticed the lunch lady. She held a mop and looked sad.

"Hey guys," Shirley said. "We can't just leave. We need to clean up the mess. After all, we're the ones who made it."

Slowly, her friends returned. They picked up the trash, cleaned the tables, and mopped the floors.

They missed recess that day. When they finally left the cafeteria, it was sparkling clean. And the lunch lady was smiling.

After Reading Activities

You and the Story...

Who started the food fight?

Why did Shirley Squirrel think it was important to clean up the mess?

Have you ever made a really big mess either at school or at home?

What was the mess and how did you clean it up?

Words You Know Now...

Many of the words below are very similar in meaning. What is unique about each one? For example, "toss" means not only to throw, but to throw lightly.

hurl	shoot
launch	soar
pitch	toss
sail	zing

You Could...Plan a Picnic with Friends

Decide on a place. It can be outside at a park or in your backyard. It can be inside on the living room floor.

Decide on a menu. Include:

- a type of sandwich everyone likes
- a fruit, like strawberries or watermelon
- potato or macaroni salad
- chips
- an easy to eat dessert, like cookies

Have each person choose an item or two and bring enough to share.

Think about what chores will need to be done. Who will set out the plates and napkins? Who will clean up the trash?

Enjoy eating your picnic food—not throwing it!

Remember to clean up your mess.

About the Author

Kyla Steinkraus lives in Tampa, Florida with her husband and two children. She thinks eating food is more fun than throwing it.

About the Illustrator

Acclaimed for its versatility in style, Anita DuFalla's work has appeared in many educational books, newspaper articles, and business advertisements and on numerous posters, book and magazine covers, and even giftwraps. Anita's passion for pattern is evident in both her artwork and her collection of 400 patterned tights. She lives in the Friendship neighborhood of Pittsburgh, Pennsylvania with her son, Lucas.